BODIES

by Barbara Brenner
with photographs
and design by
George Ancona

E. P. Dutton
New York

TEXT COPYRIGHT © 1973 BY BARBARA BRENNER
PHOTOGRAPHS COPYRIGHT © 1973 BY GEORGE ANCONA
ALL RIGHTS RESERVED. PRINTED IN THE U.S.A.

Published in the United States by E. P. Dutton,
2 Park Avenue, New York, N.Y. 10016,
a division of NAL Penguin Inc.

ISBN: 0-525-26770-0   LCC: 72-89838
10

To Dr. Alex

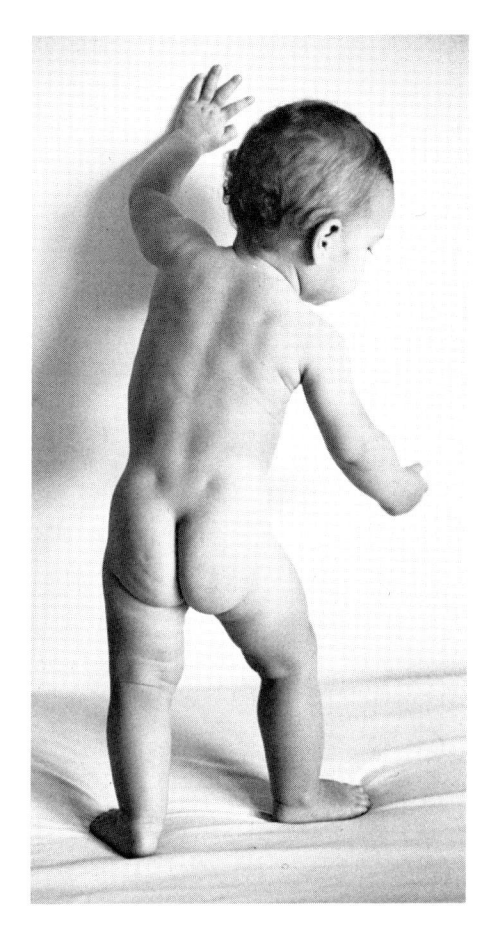

A body...

A body...

A body.

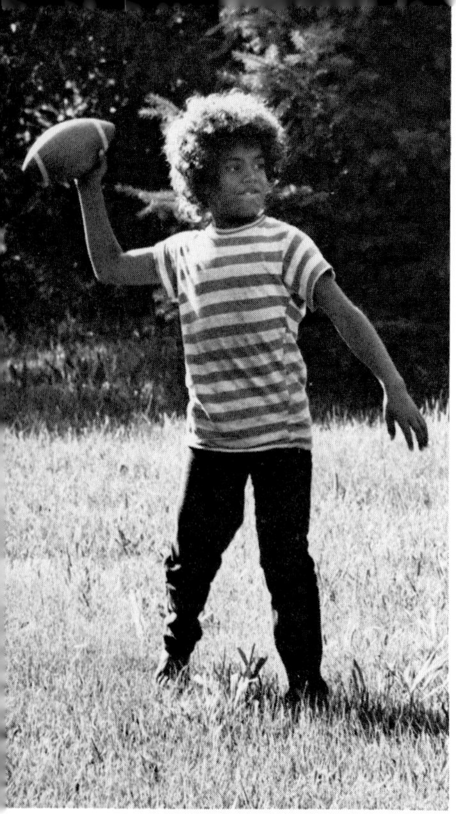
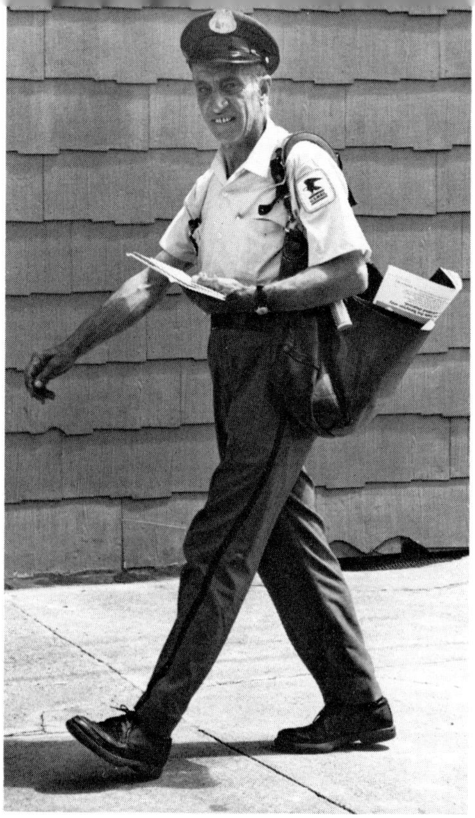
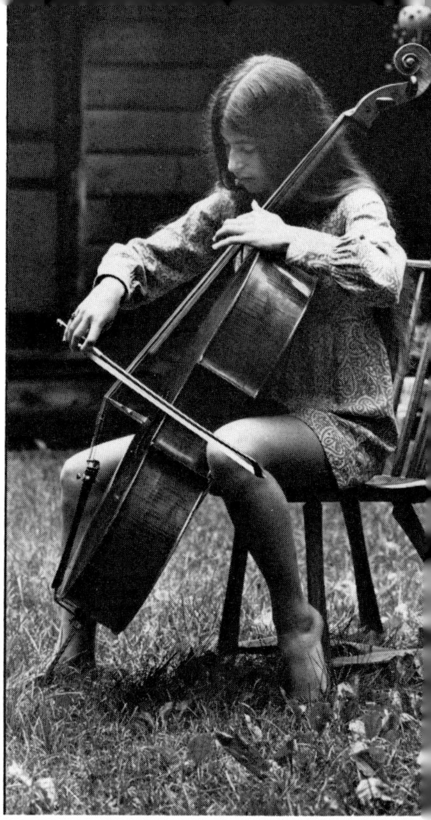
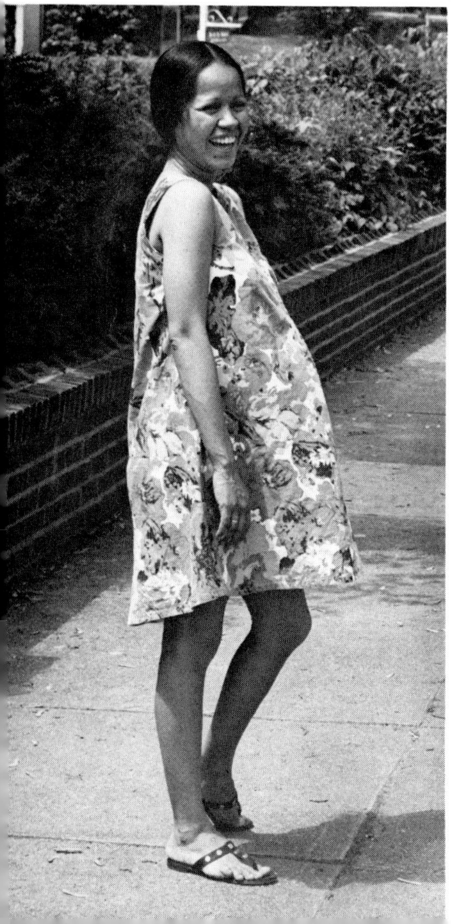
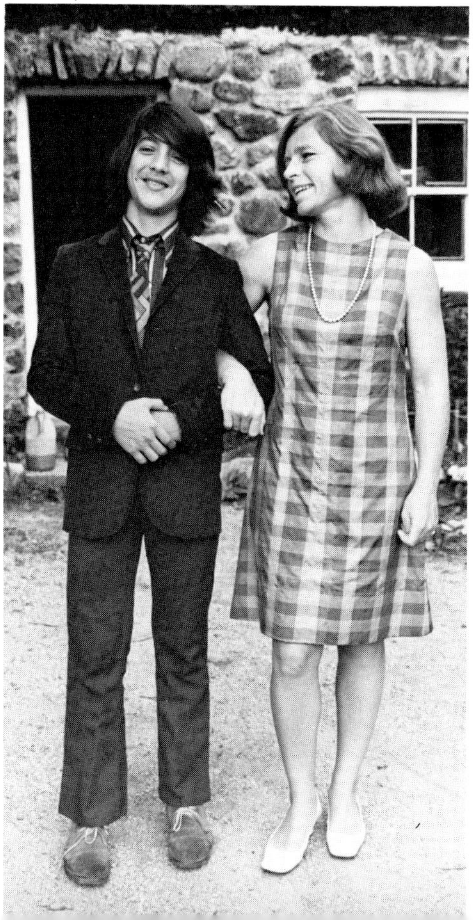
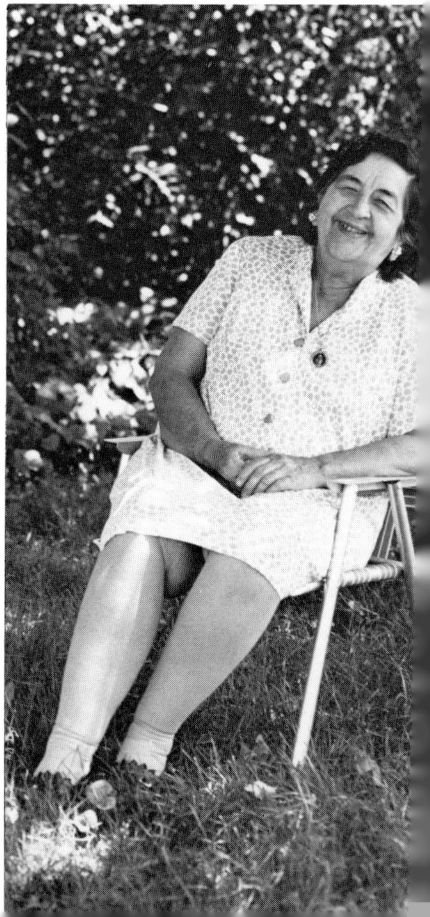

Everyone has one.

Where?
All over.
Your body's every
part of you.

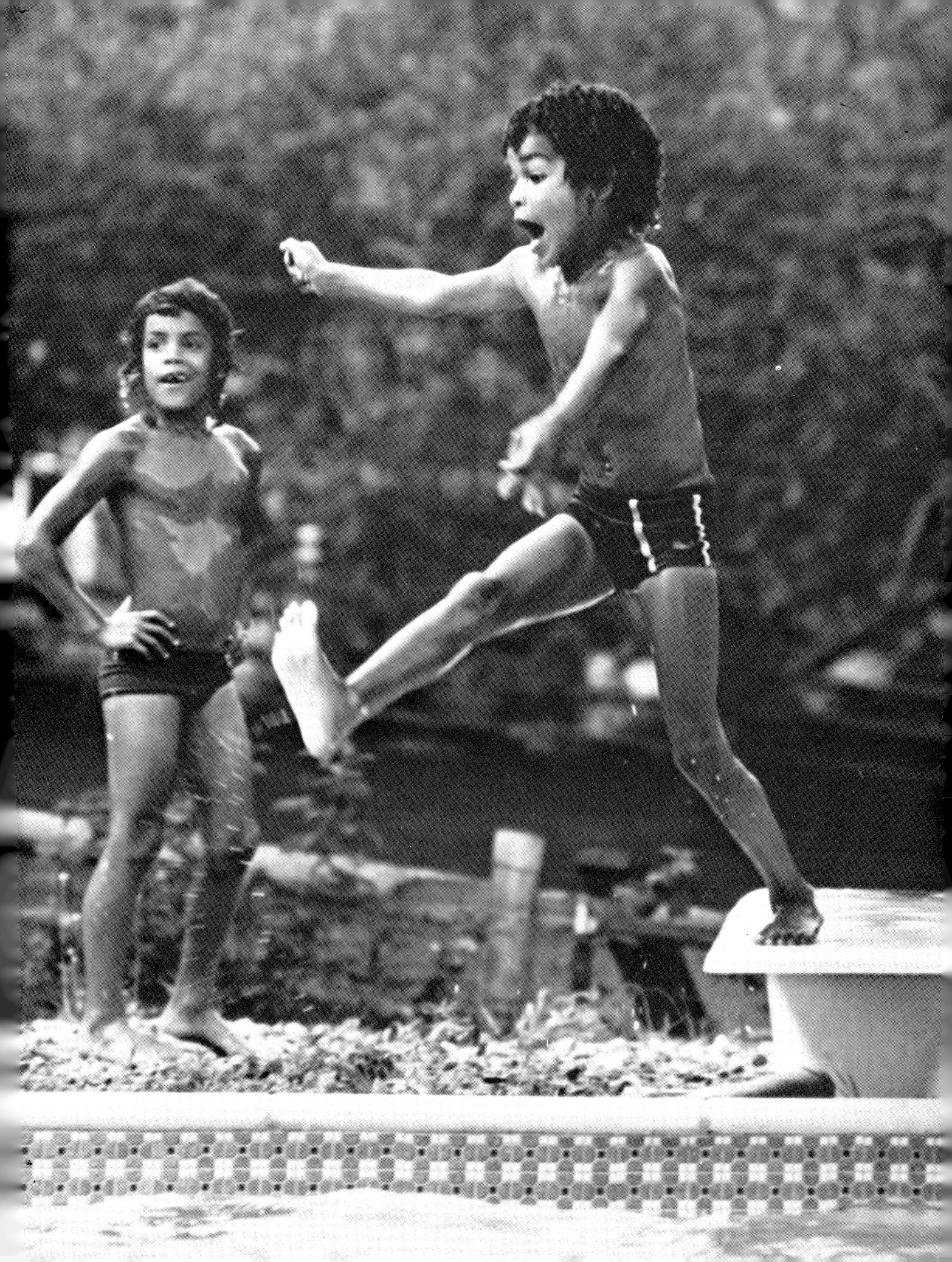

What's your body made of?

Is it made of
Glass?
Wood?
Wire?
Dough?
No.

It's made of flesh and blood
and skin and bones.

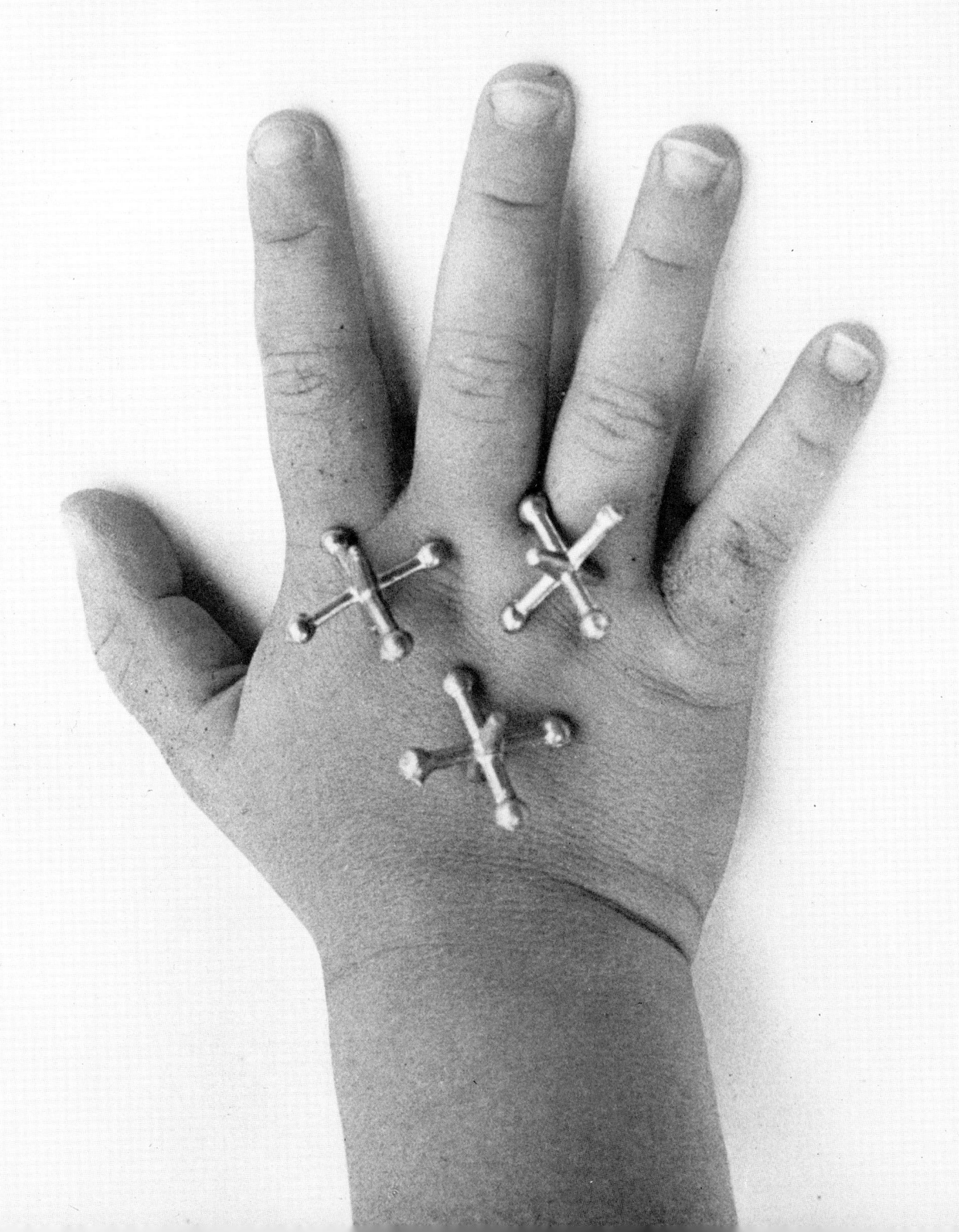

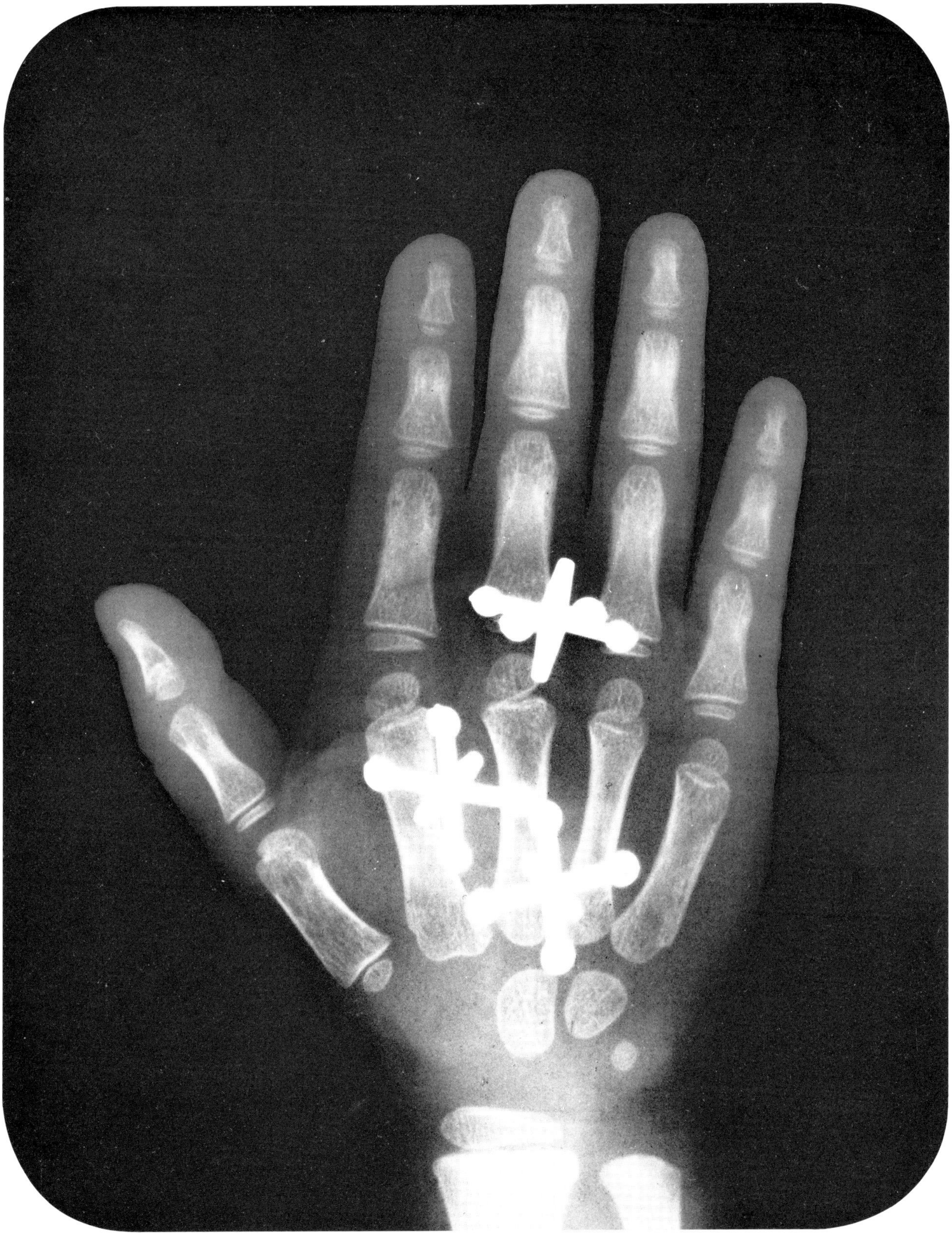

What's flesh and blood
and skin and bones made of?
Cells.
Millions of cells.
So small you can't see them.
But they're always there…
Keeping your body going,
and growing.
And each cell seems to know
how to grow.

These are blood cells
seen under a microscope.

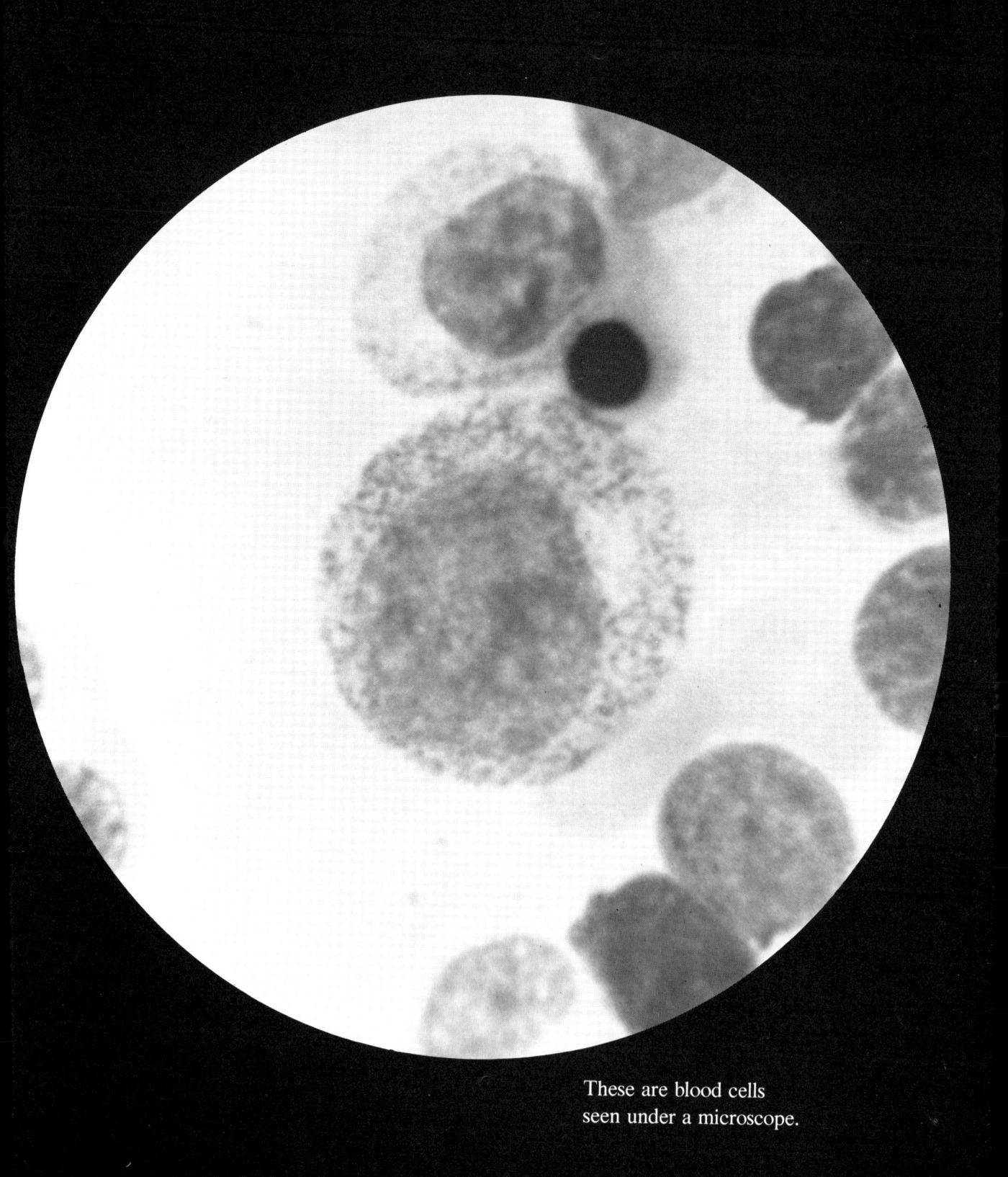

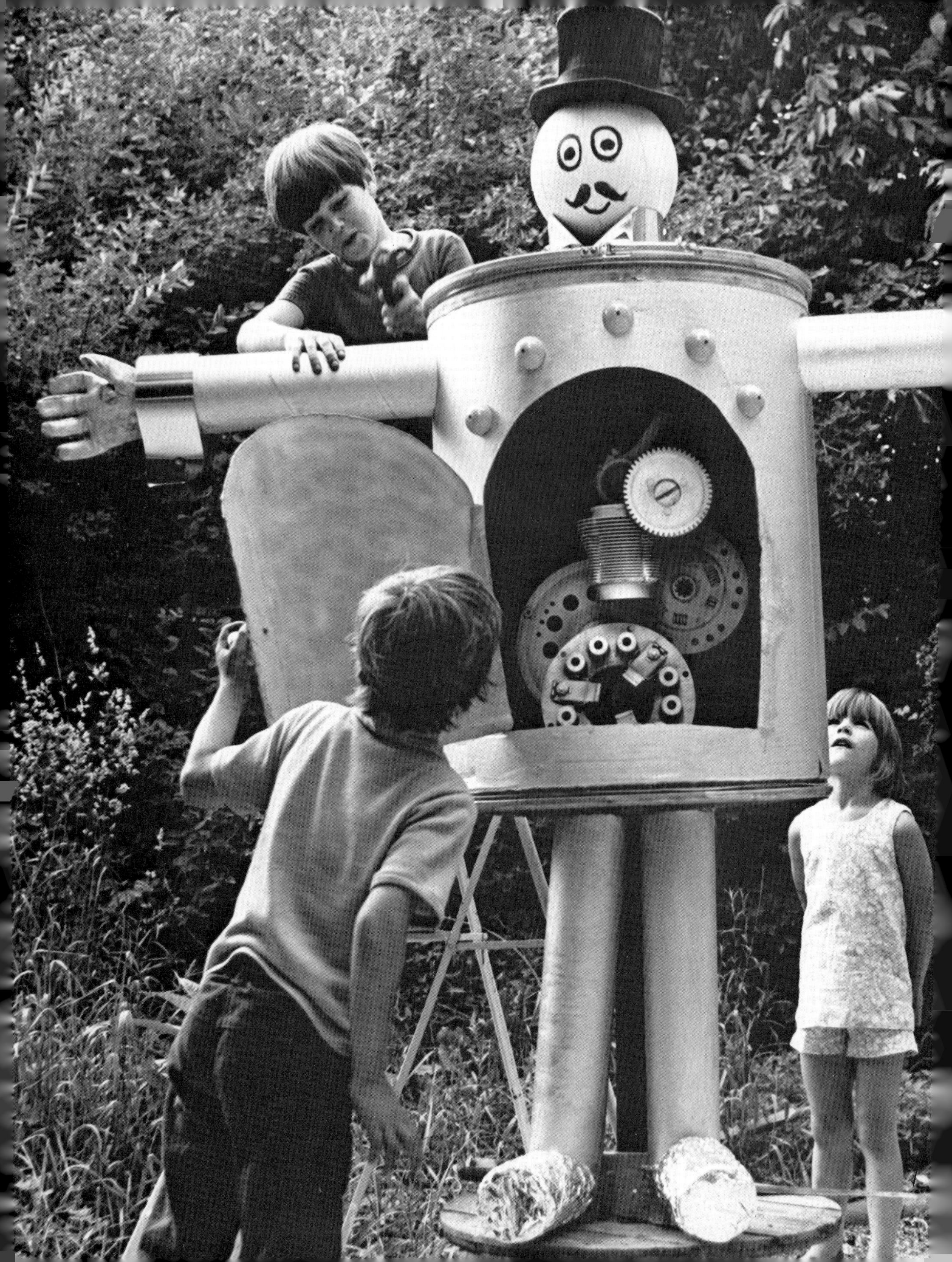

What's a body like?
Is it like a machine?
It has parts like a machine.

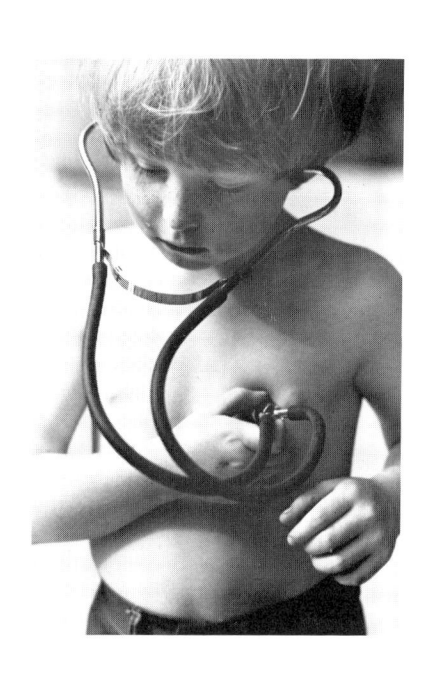

If you listen hard you hear
something ticking inside.
Like a machine.

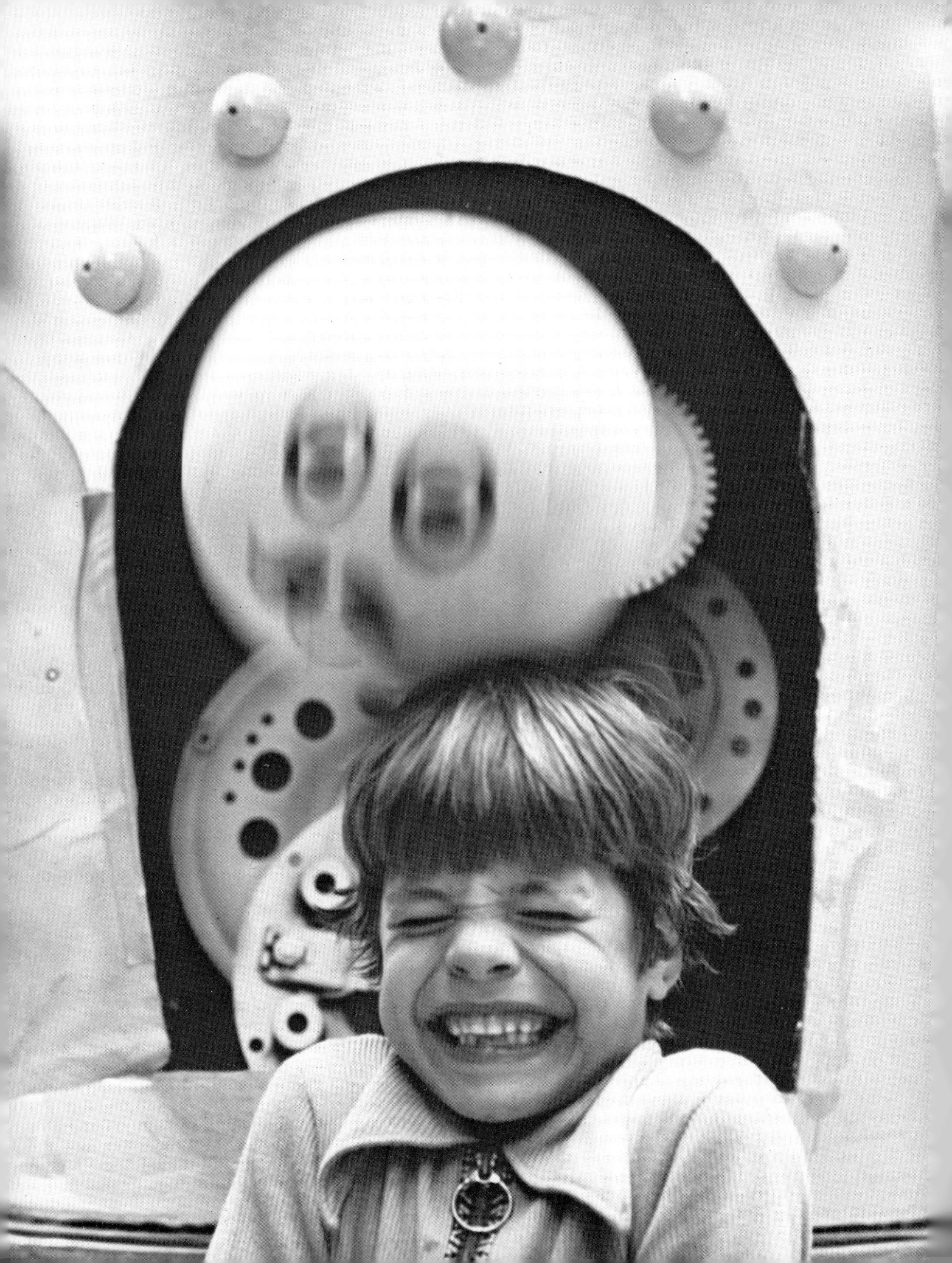

But...
A body is *alive*.
A machine isn't alive.
A body feels things.
A machine has no feelings.
So a body can't be a machine,
even though it seems
like a machine.

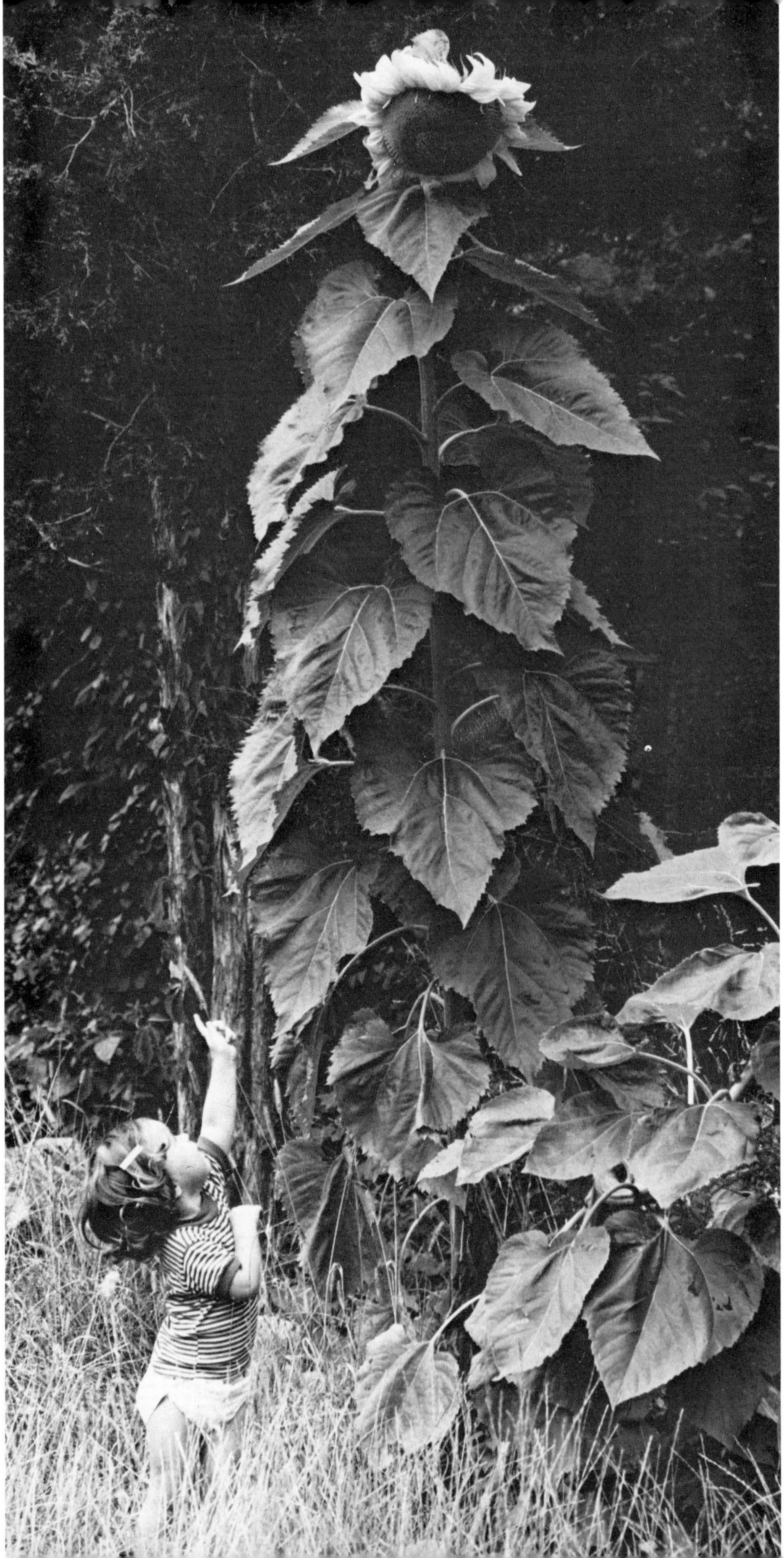

Maybe a body is
a plant.
It's alive like a plant.
It grows like a plant.
It must be a plant.
But a plant grows in dirt…
Does a body grow in dirt?

Do you water a body
to make it grow?

No!

And a body
can move from
place to place.
A plant
can't.
So a body's
not really like
a plant.

Then what is it really like?
It's alive...
It grows...
It's something like
other growing things...
But it's most like...
an animal.
Is it an animal?

Yes.
A human
animal.

Bodies.
Are they
all the same?
Some parts
look the same.

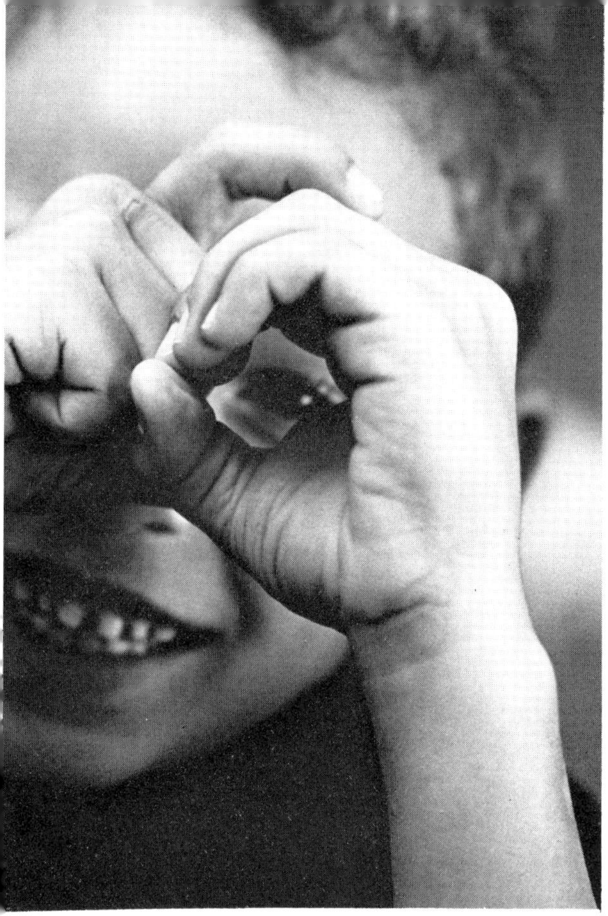
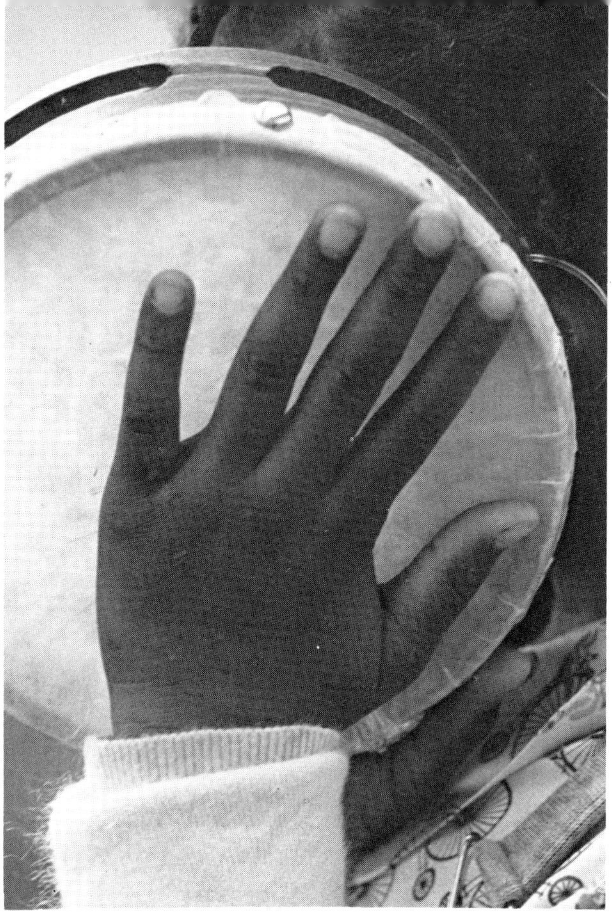
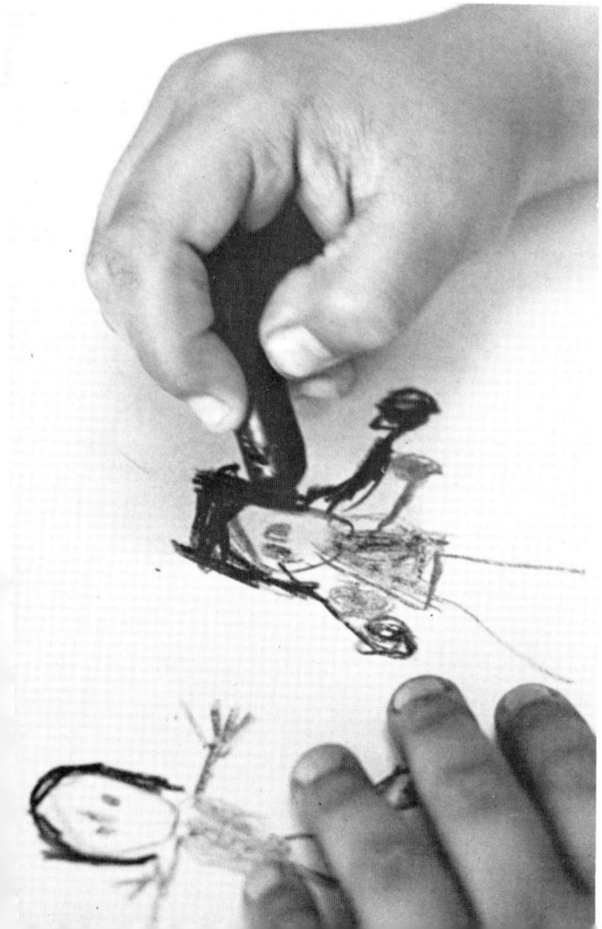
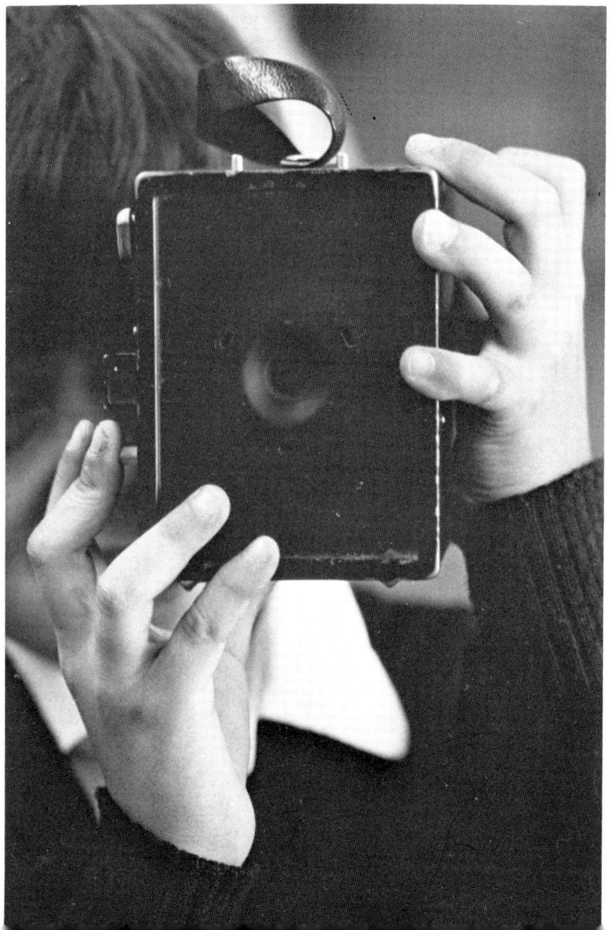

Boys look like other boys.

Girls look like other girls.

Everyone has a bellybutton.

But no two bodies are just the same. In all the world you won't find anyone who is exactly like you.

(Except...)

What do you do
with a body?
Live with it. Grow.

Breathe.   Eat.   Move.

Sweat.  Eliminate.  Sleep.

All the
things you
have to do.

What else
do you do
with your body?
All the things
you can do.
Everything
you want to do.
The things you
learn to do.
But...
Whatever
you do...

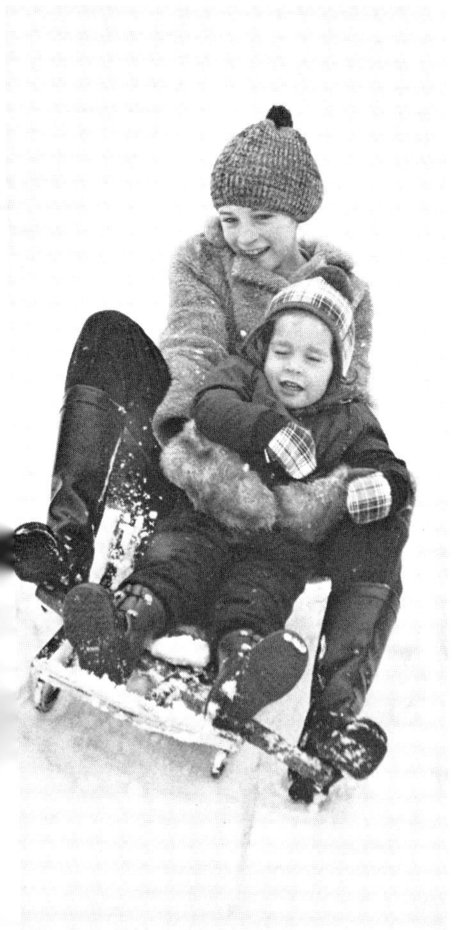
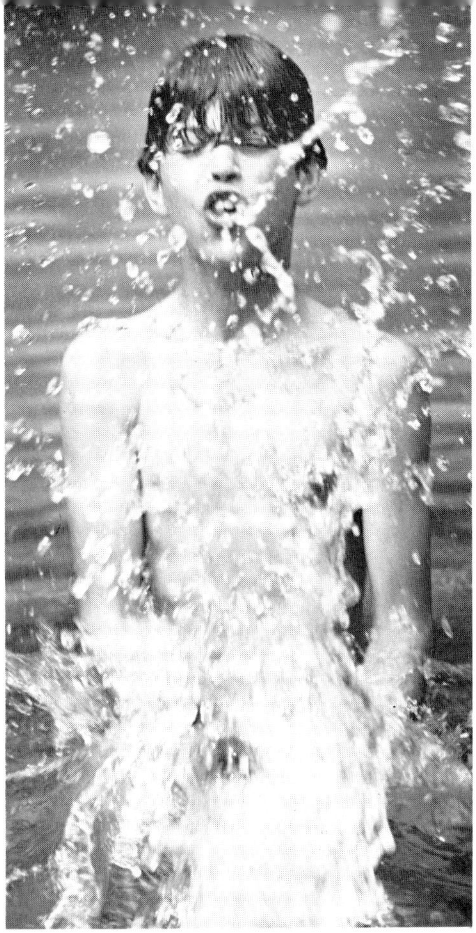
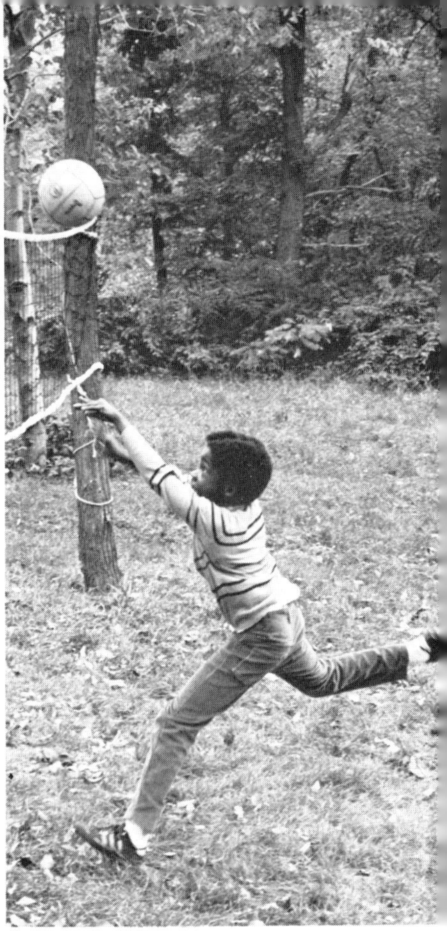
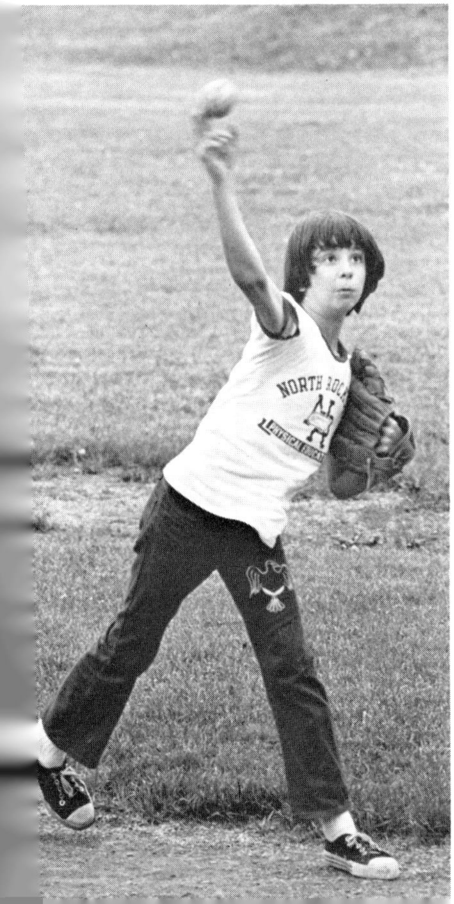
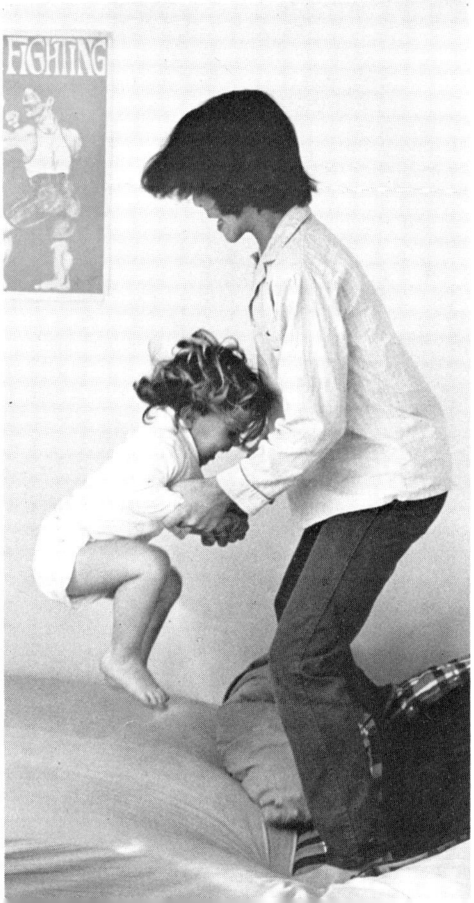
FIGHTING
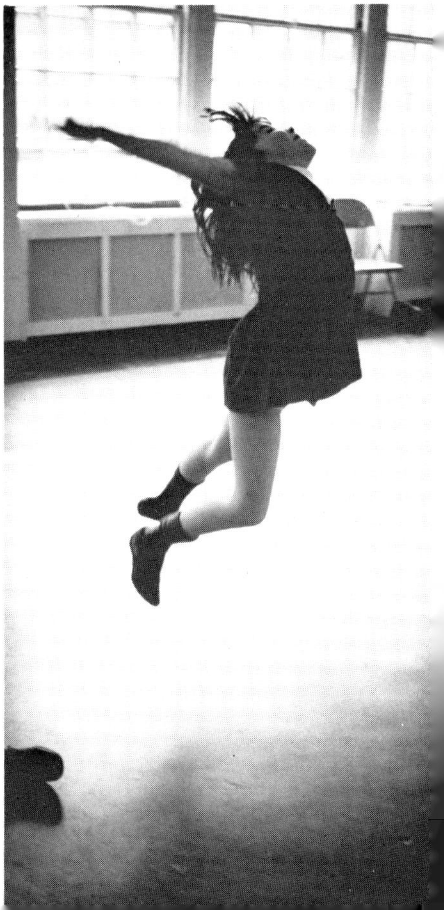

You do it your way. Not like anyone else.

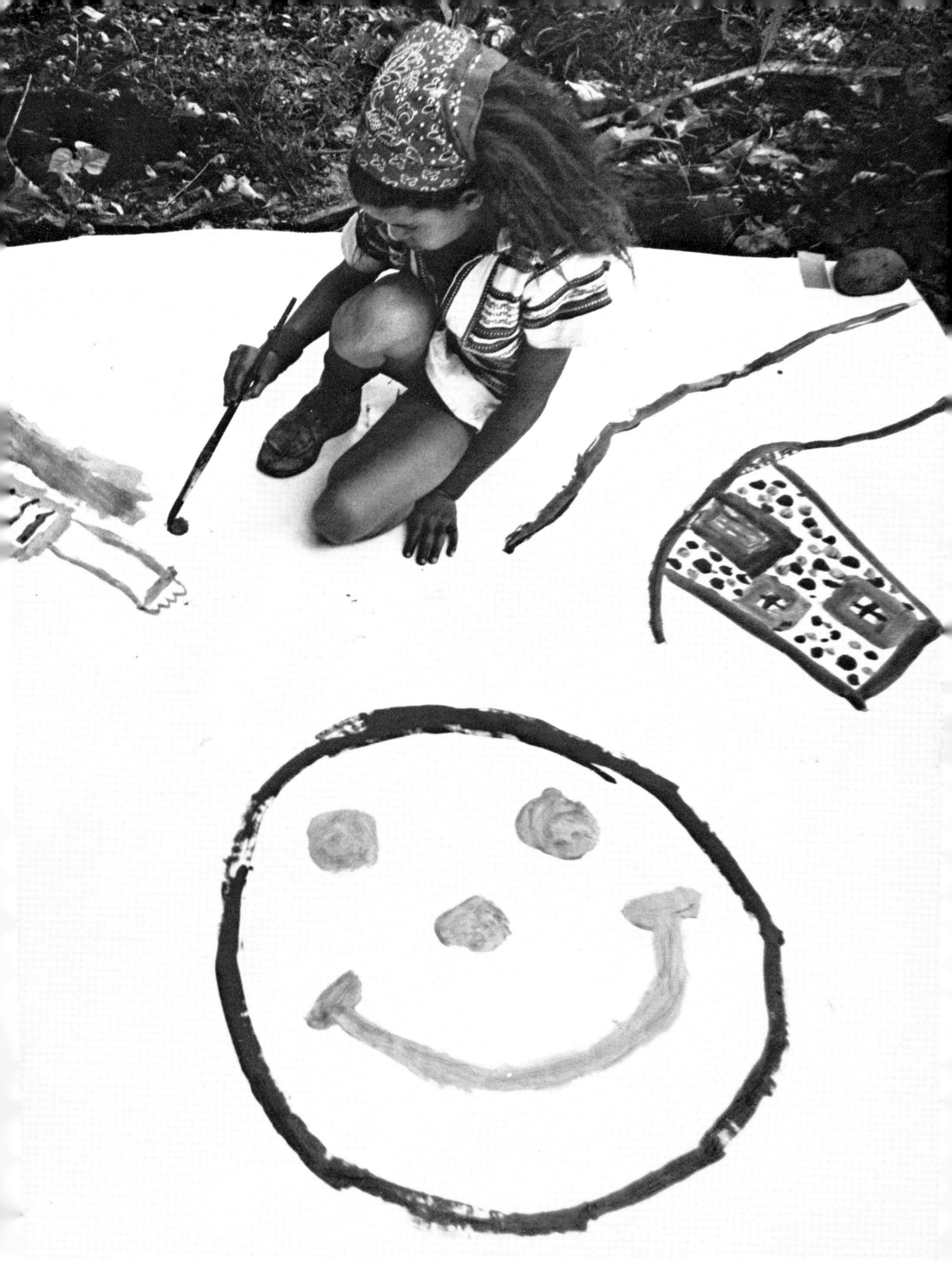

Because you're not like anyone else.

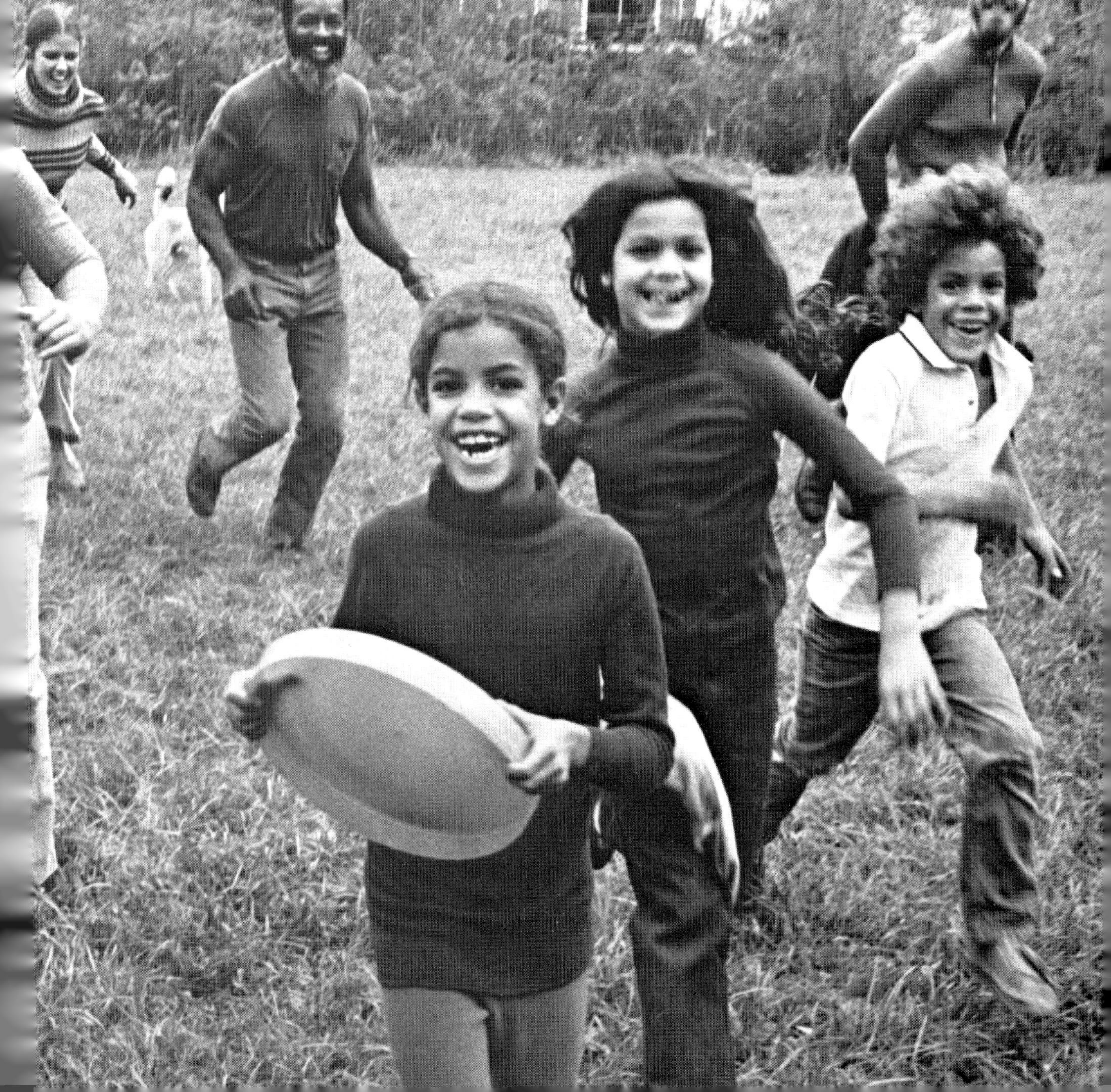

Your cells,
your fingerprints,
your face…

The color of your eyes...
They're yours alone.

And the color
of your thoughts
and dreams
is just as much
your own.

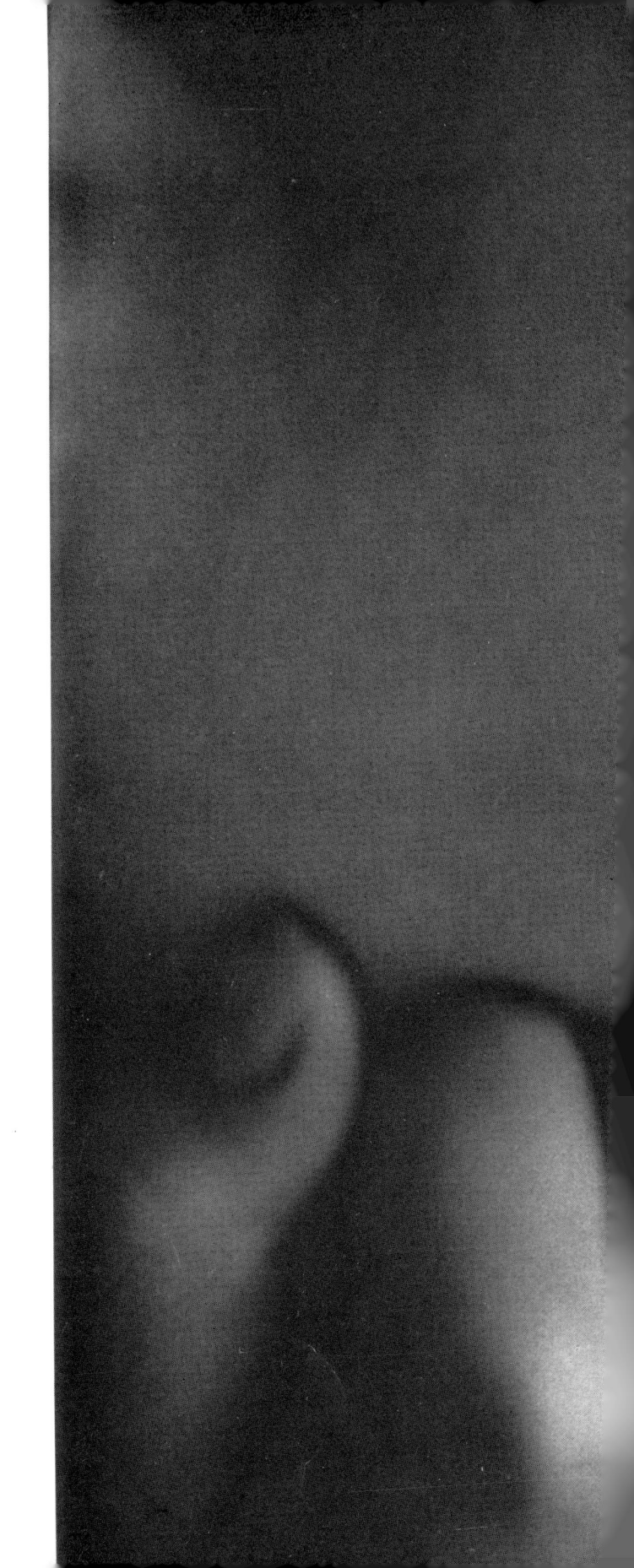

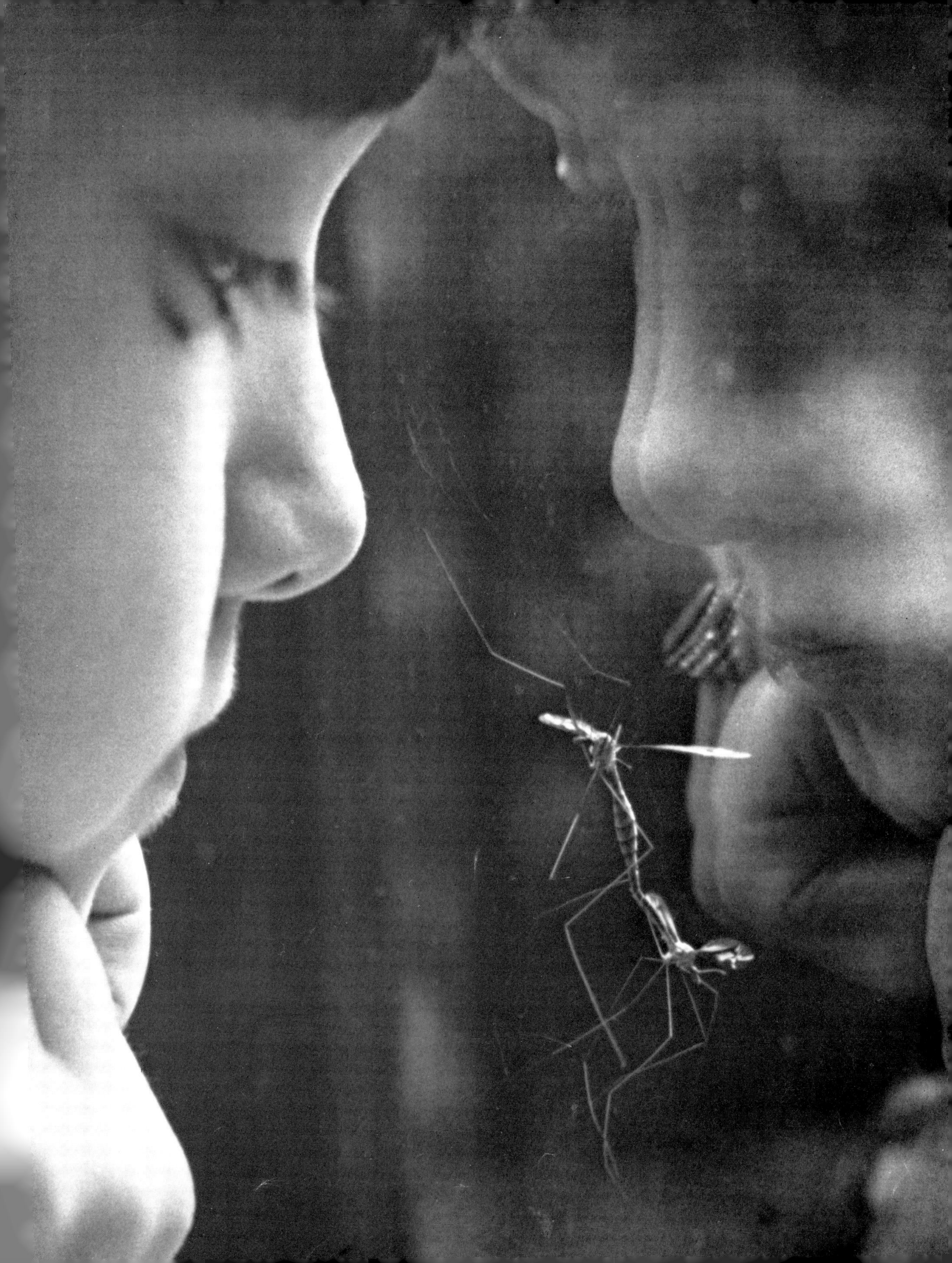

Because...

you're you.

A body and a mind.

One of a kind.

BARBARA BRENNER has written more than a dozen books for young people. Among them are *Faces* (with photographs by George Ancona), *Barto Takes the Subway* (a Herald Tribune Honor Book in 1960), *A Snake Lover's Diary* (an ALA Notable Book in 1970), and *A Year in the Life of Rosie Bernard.* Mrs. Brenner thinks it "would be nice if the sense of wonder could stay around for all of a child's life." She lives in Nyack, New York, with her husband and two sons.

GEORGE ANCONA is a photographer, graphic designer, and filmmaker. He feels that his youth in Coney Island gave him a fantastic early visual education. He studied painting in Mexico and returned to New York to attend Cooper Union and the Art Students' League. Mr. Ancona worked as an advertising art director until he decided that "photography was more fun." He lives in Stony Point, New York, with his wife and five children.